IMPRINT

A part of Macmillan Publishing Group, LLC
120 Broadway, New York, NY 10271

ABOUT THIS BOOK

The art was created with Dr. PH Martin's Watercolor, Brusho Powdered Pigment,
Prismacolor, and Polychromos Colored Pencils with Photoshop. The text was set in Intelo 20 and the
display type is Cafeteria. The book was edited by Erin Stein and designed by Carolyn Bull.
The production was supervised by Raymond Ernesto Colón and the production editor was Dawn Ryan.

Library of Congress Cataloging-in-Publication Data is available.

ISBN 978-1-250-31574-8 (hardcover)

Our books may be purchased in bulk for promotional, educational, or business use. Please contact
your local bookseller or the Macmillan Corporate and Premium Sales Department at
(800) 221-7945 ext. 5442 or by email at MacmillanSpecialMarkets@macmillan.com.

Imprint logo designed by Amanda Spielman

First edition, 2020

1 3 5 7 9 10 8 6 4 2

mackids.com

Steal this book and fear the worst,
for you will soon be gravely cursed.
Your house will fill with bats and frogs,
with polar bears and snorting hogs,
with elephants and rhinos, too,
and there will be no room for you!

WILD ABOUT DADS

WRITTEN BY DIANA MURRAY   ILLUSTRATED BY AMBER ALVAREZ

[Imprint]
MAKE YOUR MARK

NEW YORK

Dads. They go by many names
and no two dads are quite the same,

but though we see them every day . . .
what are dads like, anyway?

Dads can help you reach up high,

and help to keep you warm and dry.

Dads like fishing in the creek,

and playing games, like hide-and-seek.

Dads are strong. Dads are brave.
But sometimes . . .

. . . dads could use a shave!

Dads fetch dinner in a snap,

and like
to take a
cozy nap.

Dads are quick to share a snack

or carry you on piggyback.
And dads would rarely miss the chance . . .

to strut their stuff and dance, dance, dance!

Dads are skilled at catching bugs,

and wrapping you in great big hugs.

And when you're tired from all your play,
dads can help you find your way . . .

through the bushes, down the path.
Off to bed! But first . . . a bath.

Dads can help you touch the sky.
Spread your wings . . .

and up you fly!

There's a lot that dads can do.

The best of all is loving you!

MARMOSET dads groom, feed, and carry their babies on their backs.

EMPEROR PENGUINS live in Antarctica, the coldest place on earth. Penguin dads help keep their chicks warm on top of their feet.

EAGLE dads swoop down to catch fish and other small animals. They bring food back to the nest to feed their chicks.

PRAIRIE DOGS live in holes called burrows. Prairie dog dads help maintain and protect them.

HIPPO dads are fierce protectors of their families. Even hungry crocodiles are no match for their huge chompers!

BEARDED EMPEROR TAMARINS are known for their funny-looking facial hair. The tamarin dad and everyone in his group help to take care of the young.